dauid or

has written too many books to
count, ranging from poetry to
non-fiction.

When he is not writing he
travels around the UK, giving
performances and running
writing workshops.

David is a huge science
fiction fan and has the biggest
collection of science fiction
magazines that the Starchasers
have ever seen.

starchasers
the ultimate secret

by

david orme

illustrated by
jorge mongioui

Ransom

starchasers

The Ultimate Secret
by David Orme

Illustrated by Jorge Mongiovi

Published by Ransom Publishing Ltd.
51 Southgate Street, Winchester, Hants. SO23 9EH, UK

www.ransom.co.uk

ISBN 978 184167 766 8

First published in 2009

A CIP catalogue record of this book is available from the British Library.

misha hanson

captain

 Owner of the *Lightspinner*.

 When her rich father died, Misha could have lived in luxury – but that was much too boring.

 She spent all the money on the *Lightspinner* – and a life of adventure!

 Misha is the boss – but she doesn't always get her own way.

"Whenever we're in trouble, I know I've got a great team with me. The Starchasers will never let me down!"

DATA FILE

suma

science officer

He may look like a cat from Earth, but he is an alien with a brilliant mind for science – and sharp teeth and claws!

Probably the smartest cat in space. Finn and Misha don't need to tell him that – he knows!

Suma's not always easy to get on with. Take care – he makes a dangerous enemy!

"Misha tells people I'm just a big softy. The biggest softy in the galaxy. You know what? She's wrong."

**finn
2021**

pilot

- Finn is a great guy to have around when there's trouble – and for the Starchasers, that's most of the time.

- Probably the best pilot Planet Earth has ever produced – though Misha and Suma don't tell him that, of course!

- Finn is great for getting the Starchasers out of (and sometimes in to) trouble! If only he didn't love gadgets so much …

"I was in big trouble when Misha found me in an on-line computer game. She changed my life!"

DATA FILE

the **Light spinner**

model
Scout ship Model Q 590:
Lightspinner

date built
July, 2357

crew
Three

top speed
150 x light speed

acceleration
0 – light speed in
15.5 seconds

power
Faster than light – 2 Quantum Engines
Sub light speed – 2 Fermium Thrusters

landing craft
1 x Model LC250 Lander

communication
Spacenet™ multiphase

navigation system
R.O.B 57 series computer

> **"THE TOP-OF-THE-RANGE SOUND
> SYSTEM WILL BLOW YOUR MIND!"**
> SPACE SOUNDS APRIL 2357

"THE NEW Q590 - LIGHT SPEED IN 15.5 SECONDS - YOU'RE GONNA LOVE THIS BABY!"

WHAT SPACESHIP   JANUARY 2Ξ57

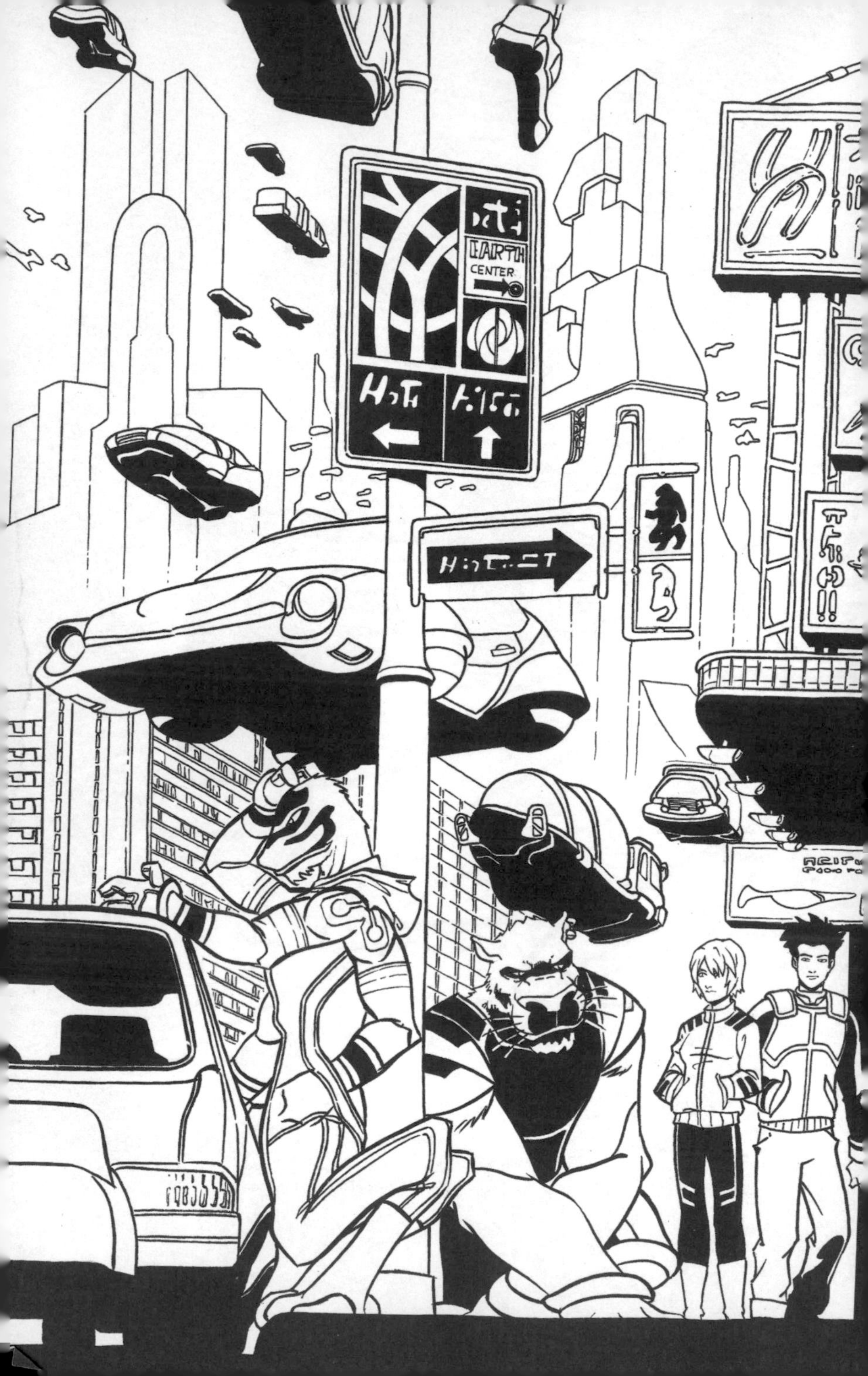
EARTH
CENTER

job done

The Starchasers had spent nearly a month on Wilson's planet. It was on the edge of the galaxy and hadn't been discovered that long ago. It was a good planet, with rich soil and plenty of useful minerals in the ground. People of many different species had come from all over the galaxy and settled there with their families.

Then the insects had arrived. They stung people, and it really hurt! The trouble was, wiping out one type of insect on a planet you didn't know was a bad idea. They might be important for things like pollinating plants.

This was just the sort of job the Starchasers were up for – the difficult jobs that no one else was able to do. Suma, their cat-like science officer, was brilliant at solving problems like this. He set up a laboratory in the main city and studied the insects. Finn was given the job of catching some of them for Suma to study. He didn't enjoy that at all!

'I can see why they hate the things!' he groaned. 'I've been bitten all over!'

Suma had found out that the insects were vital to the planet. But he was able to change their genes so their stings didn't hurt any more.

Misha and Finn were keen to get back home to Earth, but Suma had other ideas.

'There are another two planets in the life-zone round this star, but there's no life on either of them! I'd like to check them out. Is that O.K.?'

'But why, if there's no life?'

'There should be! That's why I want to go and look.'

The life-zone was the area of space around a star where life could survive – not too hot, not too cold, so there could be liquid water. When the Starchasers' ship, Lightspinner, went in to orbit around the first of the mystery planets, the bare rock and thin atmosphere told them that there was no life there – but there had been once!

'Buildings!' said Suma. 'Lots of them!'

Right across the planet they could see ruins – buildings, roads, even a ruined spaceport. People had once lived here. But where were they now?

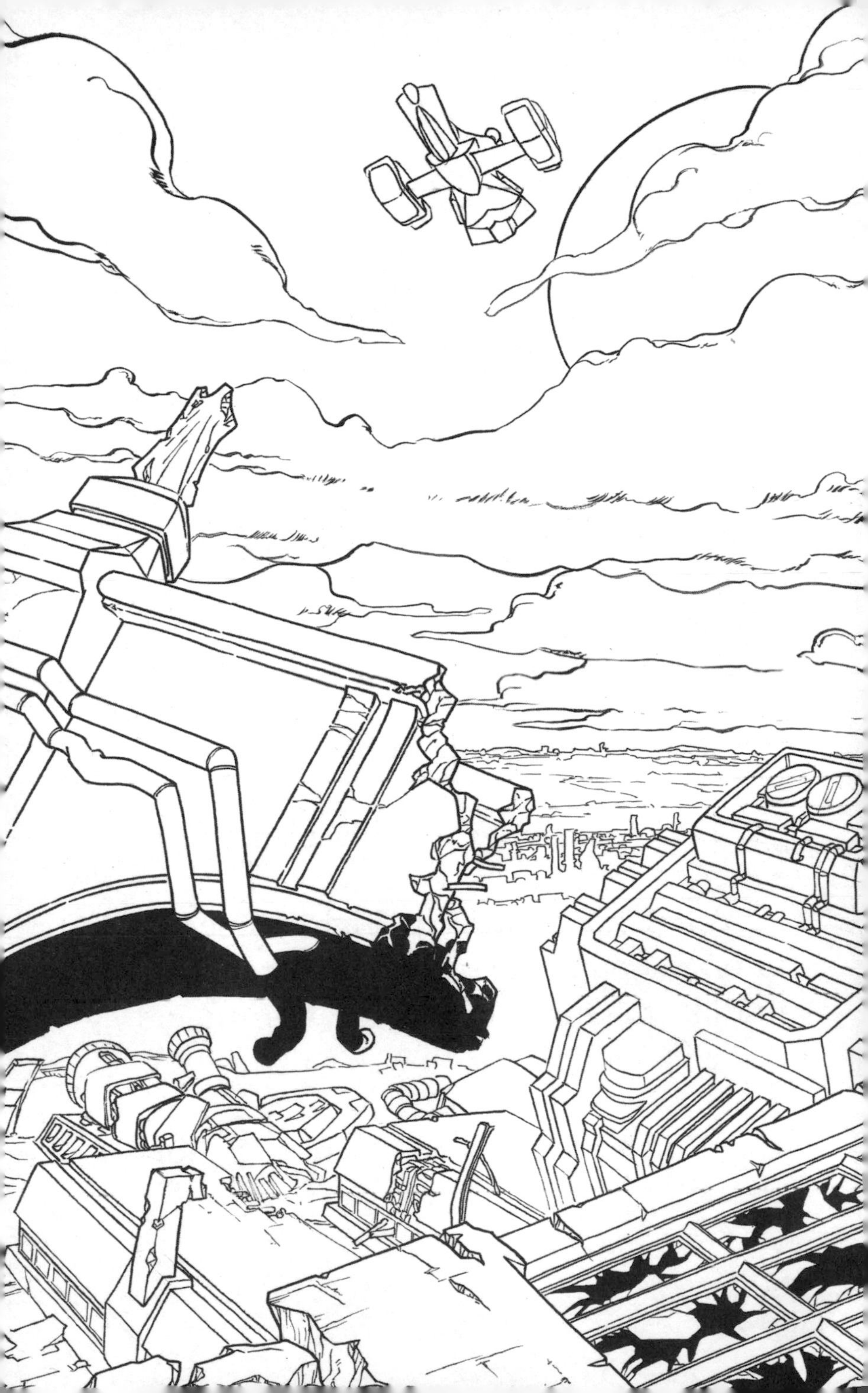

big city

'Do you want to land, Suma?'

'Let's check out the other planet first.'

A few hours later, the Lightspinner was in orbit around the second planet. It was just like the first – bare rocks, thin air and ruined buildings.

'Which planet do you want to go for, Suma?'

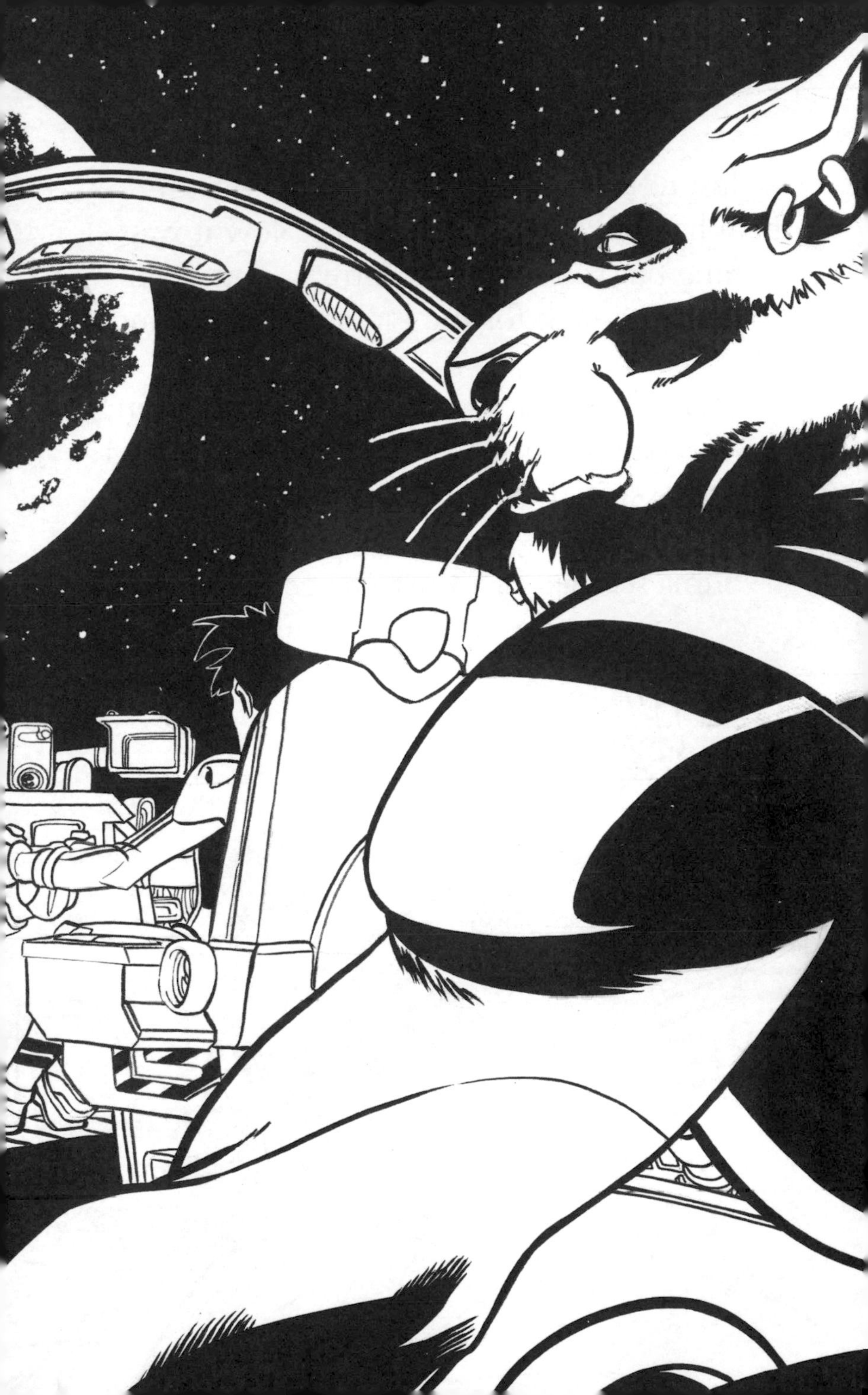

'This one. I've got a feeling about it.'

Just to the north of the planet's equator there had once been a great city. Now it was nothing but ruins. In the centre was an open space big enough for the Lightspinner to land.

'The air is bad,' said Suma. 'It's very thin, and has dangerous gases in it. We don't need full space suits, but we'll need air helmets.'

Suma seemed in a hurry to get exploring.

'What's the rush, Suma?' said Misha. 'It will be night soon. Wouldn't it be better to wait until the sun is up before we go out?'

'You're right,' said Suma. 'It's just – I told you, I've got a very strange feeling about this planet.'

'What sort of feeling?'

Suma wouldn't say. But his whiskers were twitching.

As soon as the sun was up, the Starchasers started exploring the city. The only sound was a thin wind blowing down the streets. Nothing lived on the planet now except a few scrubby plants that had adapted to the thin air.

Suma seemed even more excited. He rushed from building to building. The hair on his body was almost standing on end.

'What is it Suma?'

'Sorry, guys. I don't know why, but I just feel that I know this place.'

Finn found part of a skeleton. There were just a few bones left, tucked in a doorway, out of the wind.

Suma scanned them.

'Over a hundred thousand years old,' he said. 'Whatever happened on this planet, it was a long time ago.'

Misha shone a light through the door of a building. Everything had turned to dust – except for one thing, glittering in the light.

It was a small, stone carving of Suma.

suma's story

Suma was a very strong character. Usually he didn't show his feelings. But this time he did. Through their spacesuit radios, Finn and Misha heard a deep, sobbing howl.

'What is it, Suma? What's the matter?'

But Suma wasn't able to speak.

The Starchasers cut short the expedition and went back to the Lightspinner. Suma

disappeared into his cabin. Hours later, he came out again.

'I'm sorry guys,' he said. 'I guess I owe you an explanation.

'I've not told you much about the history of my species, though you probably know that there aren't many of us left in the galaxy.

'Humans call us the cat people, and that's fine because our real name is difficult to say. Sometimes people ask us where our home planet is, and the answer is – we just don't know!

'My species is now scattered all over the galaxy. We have no idea what planet we started out on, or why we left it. For thousands of years we have looked for our home planet. Guys, I think we've found that planet.'

'What about the other dead world?'

'No idea. But that wasn't our planet. The buildings looked all wrong.'

'What can we do to help, Suma?' asked Misha.

'I know how much you want to get back to Earth, but I'd like to stay around a little, find out a bit more. Is that O.K.?'

'I'm happy to stay as long as you need,' said Finn. 'Anyway, you cat guys are smart. We might find some secrets here even *you* don't know about!'

the aliens

To the south of the great ruined city was a high hill, with a large building on top. It didn't seem to be as badly damaged as the other buildings. Suma thought it would be a good place to explore.

They flew the lander across to it.

'Hey, looks like we've got company. That lander's got my parking place!'

There was a wide square in front of the big building. Another lander was parked in the middle of it.

Finn dropped down next to it, and the team put on their helmets.

'What do you reckon, Finn?'

'Never seen anything like it before. Alien stuff, I reckon. Doesn't look very up to date, though.'

'Keep sharp, everybody,' said Misha. 'Looks like they may still be around.'

The building had a huge door. Around it there were marks carved into the stone. Suma's whiskers were twitching again.

'That's our old language. There are only tiny scraps of it left now.'

'Can you read it?'

'No. I know a few words, but that's it. There's no one left that can speak it now. Remember, this place is over a hundred thousand years old! Until now we were a species with no history.'

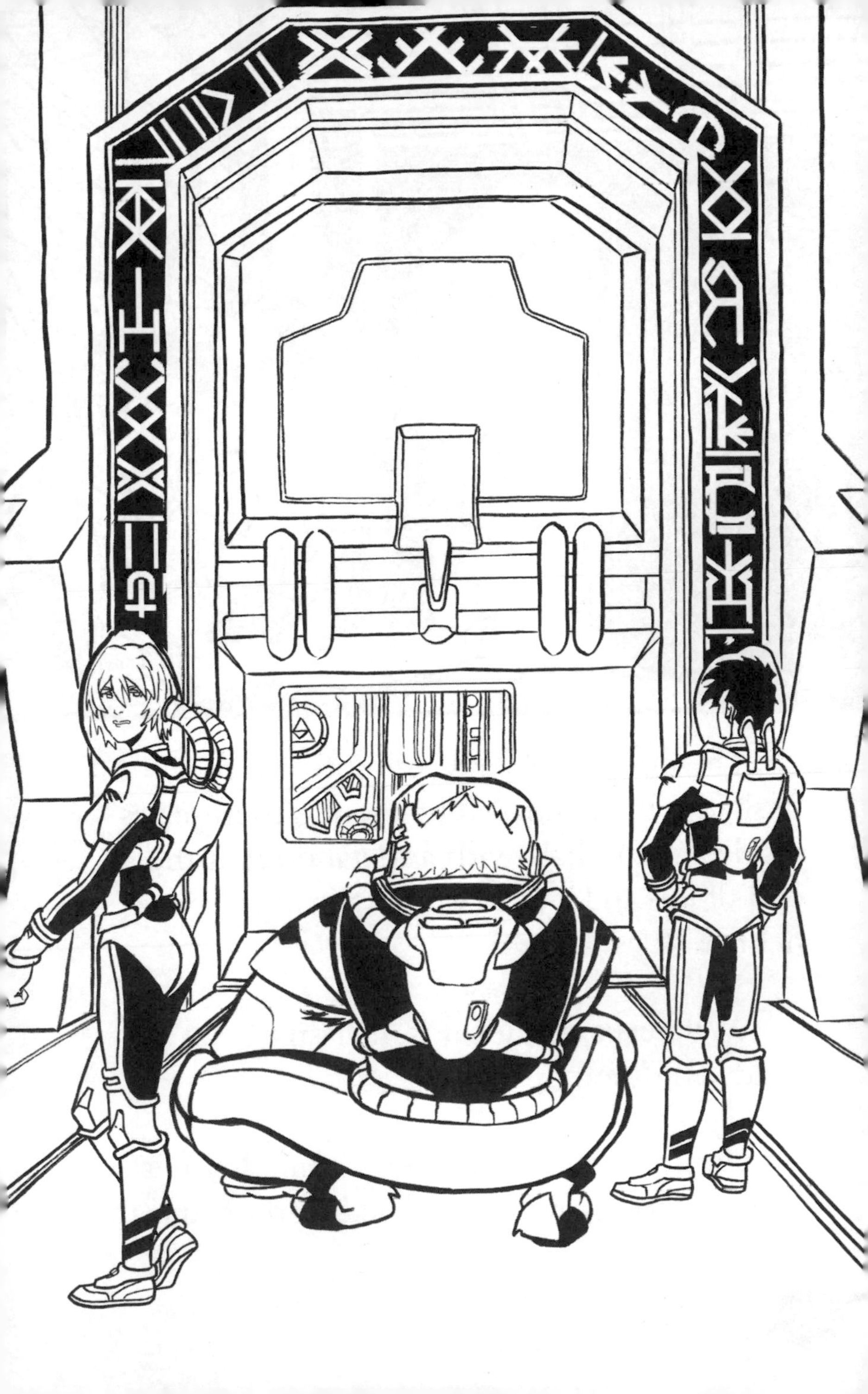

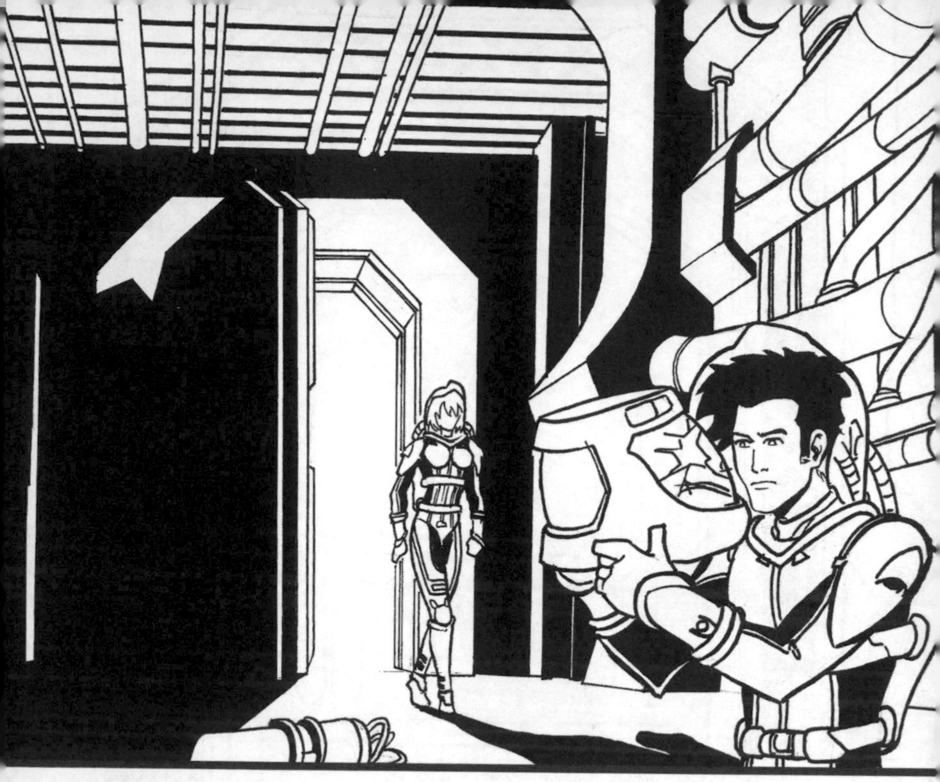

The door was heavy and stiff, but they pushed it open at last. They found themselves inside a grand hall, with a metal door at the end of it – and a dead body wearing a space helmet.

'Whatever species it is, it hasn't been dead long,' said Suma.

Finn pulled off the alien's space helmet. Its head was brown, like dried leather, and it

had no hair. Its eyes and mouth were quite human, but it had no nose.

'Don't know the species,' said Suma. 'Of course, most of this part of the galaxy is unexplored. New species keep turning up.'

'Not many of them have space flight, though,' said Misha.

It looked as if the alien had been trying to open the big metal door. Suma checked it out.

'This is amazing!' he said. 'This door is a hundred thousand years old, but everything still works. This guy was killed by an electric shock when he touched the door handle.'

'Doesn't sound as if it's working that well to me,' said Finn. 'Unless they just weren't very keen on strangers knocking on their door. Wouldn't want to deliver the mail on this planet.'

Suma was going to be very rude to Finn and explain about the door, but he forgot all about doing that when the heavily armed aliens turned up.

gunpoint

They were the same species as the alien that lay dead on the floor.

'That's a bit awkward,' whispered Misha. 'They'll think we killed him!'

That's exactly what they thought. They lined the three Starchasers up against the wall and pointed their menacing-looking weapons at them.

Then the alien who seemed to be in charge spotted the metal door. He worked out what had happened in his mind – and got it completely wrong. His man had wanted to open the door. These three weird-looking aliens must have killed him to stop him doing that. They must know what is in there – and that it's worth having!

He barked out an order. One of the aliens set off – to open the door!

'Hey, don't touch that door! It'll kill you!'

But the aliens had no idea what Finn was saying. They wouldn't have believed him if they had. The alien grabbed the door handle, there was a flash and a bang, and he dropped dead on the floor.

Once more, the chief of the aliens thought it was the Starchasers' fault. They must have booby-trapped the door.

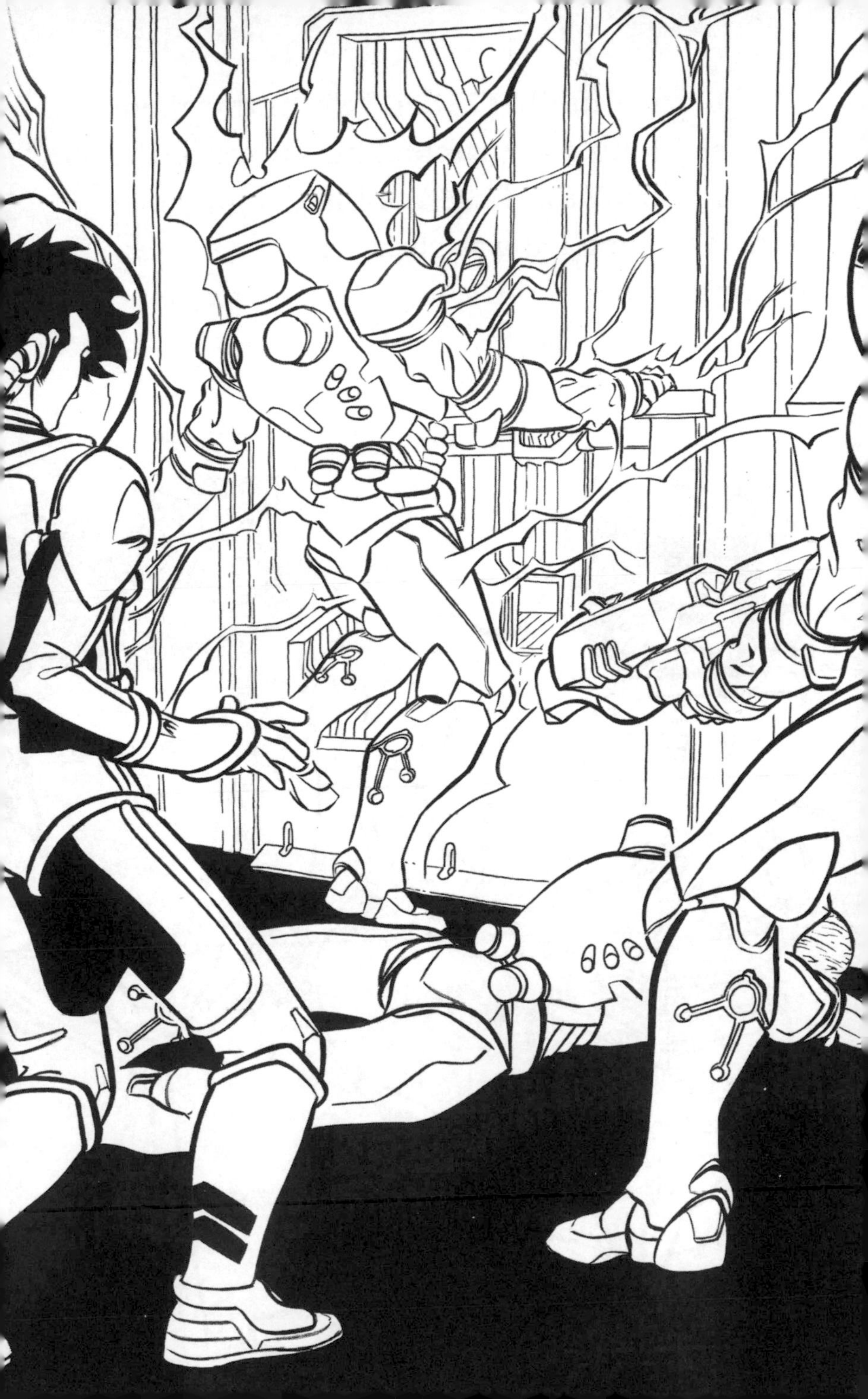

He gave another order. Two of the aliens grabbed Finn and marched him towards the metal door. A third alien pointed a gun at him. The message was clear – now it's your turn to sizzle!

Finn hesitated. The alien with the gun looked threatening. Slowly, slowly, Finn moved his hand towards the door handle, ready to snatch it away at the flashing spark.

His fingertips touched the handle. Nothing. He held it tight. A merry little tune played, and the door swung open.

'Thought that might happen,' Suma called over. 'The door's got a DNA detector. It's usually used as a lock. It only opens for the right people. It's amazing that it's still working after a hundred thousand years! It likes *you*, but it doesn't like this lot!'

'Can't tell you how pleased I am that it likes me!' said Finn.

the movie

The aliens were nervous about what might be in the room. They waved their guns at the Starchasers.

'Looks like they want us to go first,' said Misha. 'How polite of them!'

The Starchasers went in to the room. It was like a small movie theatre, with a big screen on the wall. The chief alien followed them in, but then there was a problem. The

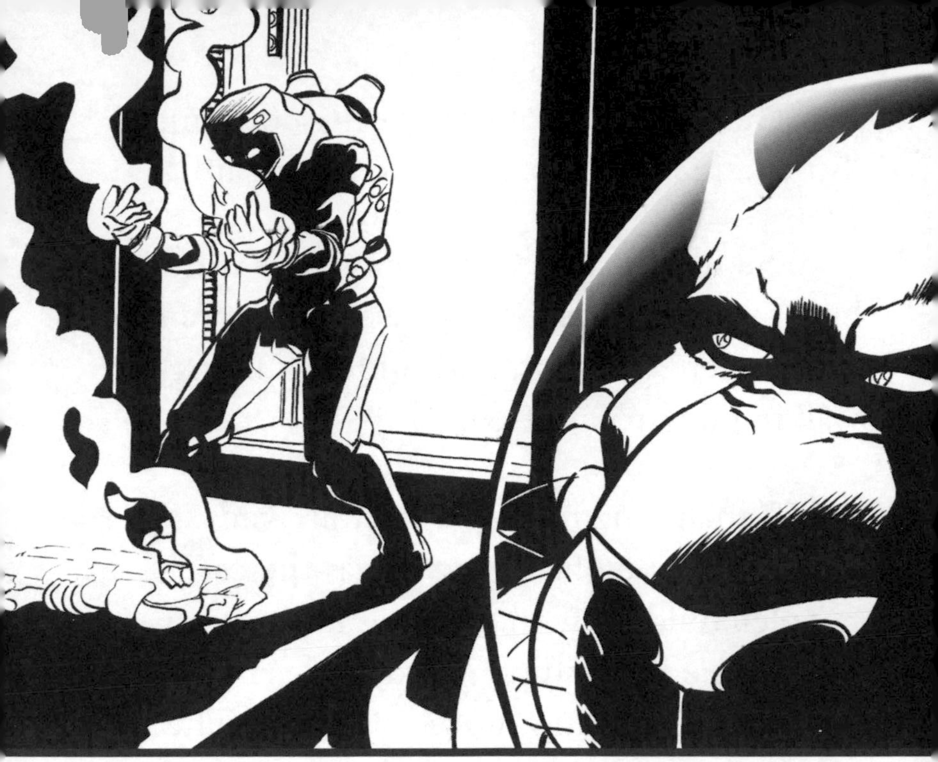

alien that came next dropped his gun with a yell. It had become red hot!

'Weapon scanner,' said Finn. 'Suma, you guys had some great technology all that time ago!'

The other aliens didn't want burnt fingers, or to give up their guns, so they stayed outside. Then the screen lit up.

'The movie's about to start!' said Finn. 'So where's the lady with the ice-cream?'

The screen showed the city they were in, but it wasn't ruined. There were cat people everywhere, going in and out of buildings, walking down the streets.

Then an enemy battle fleet arrived. Bombs dropped from the sky, as the cat people could be seen running in terror. A great space battleship landed, and armed aliens came out and started shooting. The movie zoomed in on them. Leathery face, no hair, no nose …

With a snarl, Suma leapt at the alien chief. The chief tried to fight him off, but Suma was a deadly fighter. Alarmed, the aliens outside dropped their guns and rushed to the door. Two of them got stuck in the doorway, but at last they were in. Even Suma couldn't beat that many people. They dragged him out.

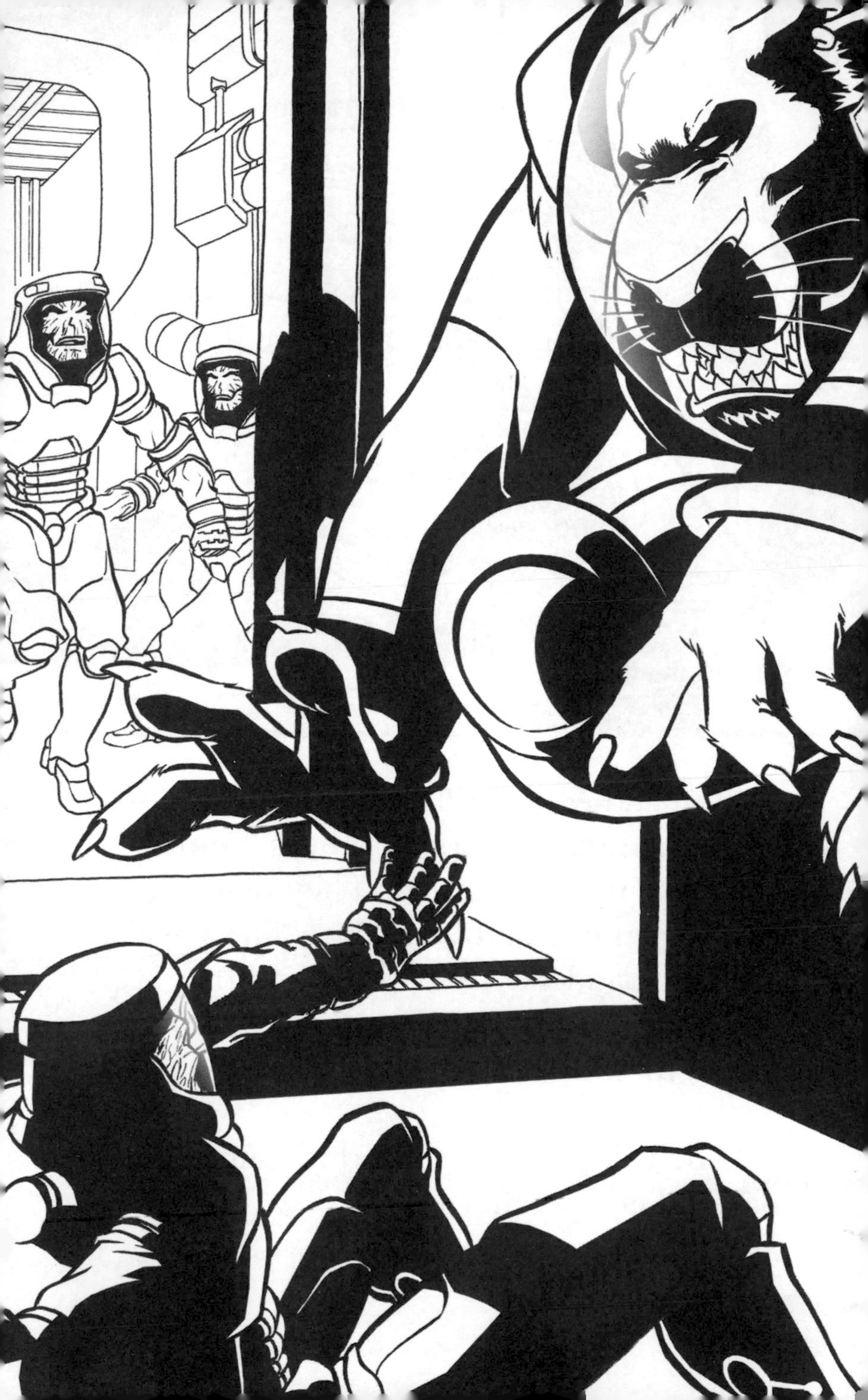

Finn and Misha followed, shouting, but the aliens took no notice of them. Suma was their enemy, not them. They dragged the cat man out of the building. There were two more landers outside now, and they pushed him into one of them. The three landers took off.

'Their ship must be in orbit!' said Finn angrily. 'Let's get after them!'

But Misha wouldn't let him.

'Finn, what can we do against heavily-armed soldiers? No. I've got a better idea. Let's get back to the Lightspinner. I want to go and look at that other ruined planet.'

'But why?'

'I told you. I've got an idea. That's all I'm saying.'

'they started it'

The alien ship was still in orbit around the cat–people planet when the Lightspinner returned from the second ruined planet. Finn piloted the Lightspinner in to orbit next to it. Then Misha called them on the radio.

'I don't suppose they will be able to understand me, but we'll have to give it a go.'

At last, the suspicious face of one of the

leathery aliens appeared on the screen. Somehow, the alien was able to speak the Common Galactic Language. Misha guessed that they had used a mind probe on Suma.

'What do you want?'

'We want our friend back.'

'Not possible. He is our enemy. We have only just found our home planet. His people destroyed our planet. We had to find a new planet to live on, light-years away. If he is your friend, you must be our enemies too. Go away!'

'But your lot destroyed his people's planet!' said Finn.

'This is true. But … they started it.'

Misha groaned. When it came to squabbles, Earth people were bad enough, but the cat people and this lot …

Then Misha had another idea.

'O.K., we'll go. But before we go, just get your captain to look at this.'

'What are you going to show them?' whispered Finn.

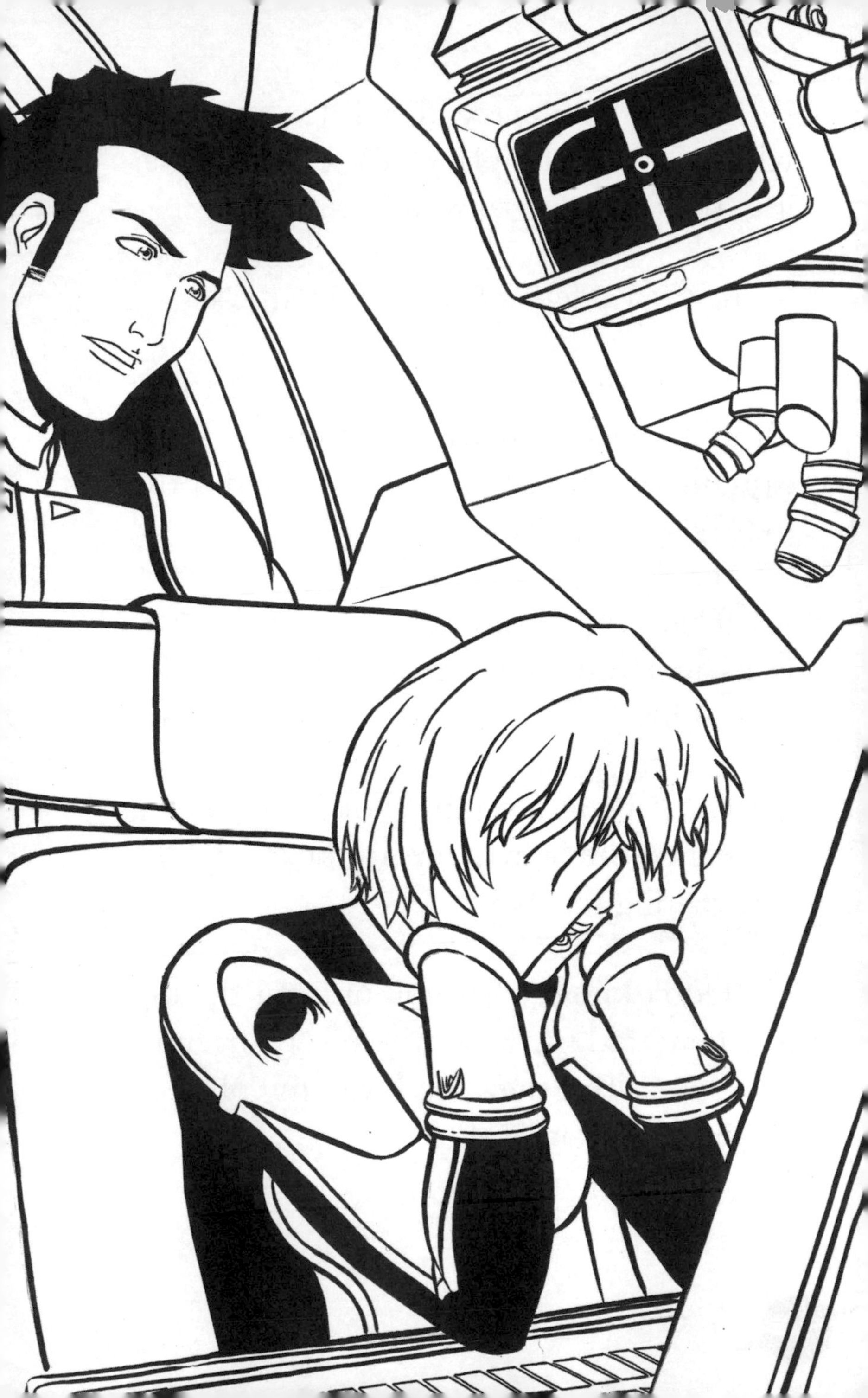

'Maybe it's a crazy idea. I don't know what's on Wilson's planet TV, but whatever it is, they're going to watch it!'

It was a celebrity game show.

'So, in the rest of the galaxy, all the different species work together?' the alien captain said at last. 'Just like they did on that terrible TV show?'

'That's right. And just a hundred or so years ago, some of them were busy killing each other!'

The captain thought about it. And at last he invited the Starchasers on board. Suma was waiting for them.

'Don't know what you did, but the big guy here told me he wanted to be friends!' said Suma. 'But they destroyed my planet! So there's no chance!'

'Suma, you'll either make friends, or …
we'll be forced to make you watch a
celebrity game show!'

Suma thought about it.

'All right then. I'll be friends. But let's get one thing clear. They started it!'

'So what did you find on the other ruined planet?' asked Suma.

'We found out it was the home planet of the people who captured you. And we watched a movie showing the cat people arriving and blasting their planet.'

'So who did start it?'

Misha sighed. 'SUMA, IT WAS A HUNDRED THOUSAND YEARS AGO. IT DOESN'T MATTER! O.K.?'

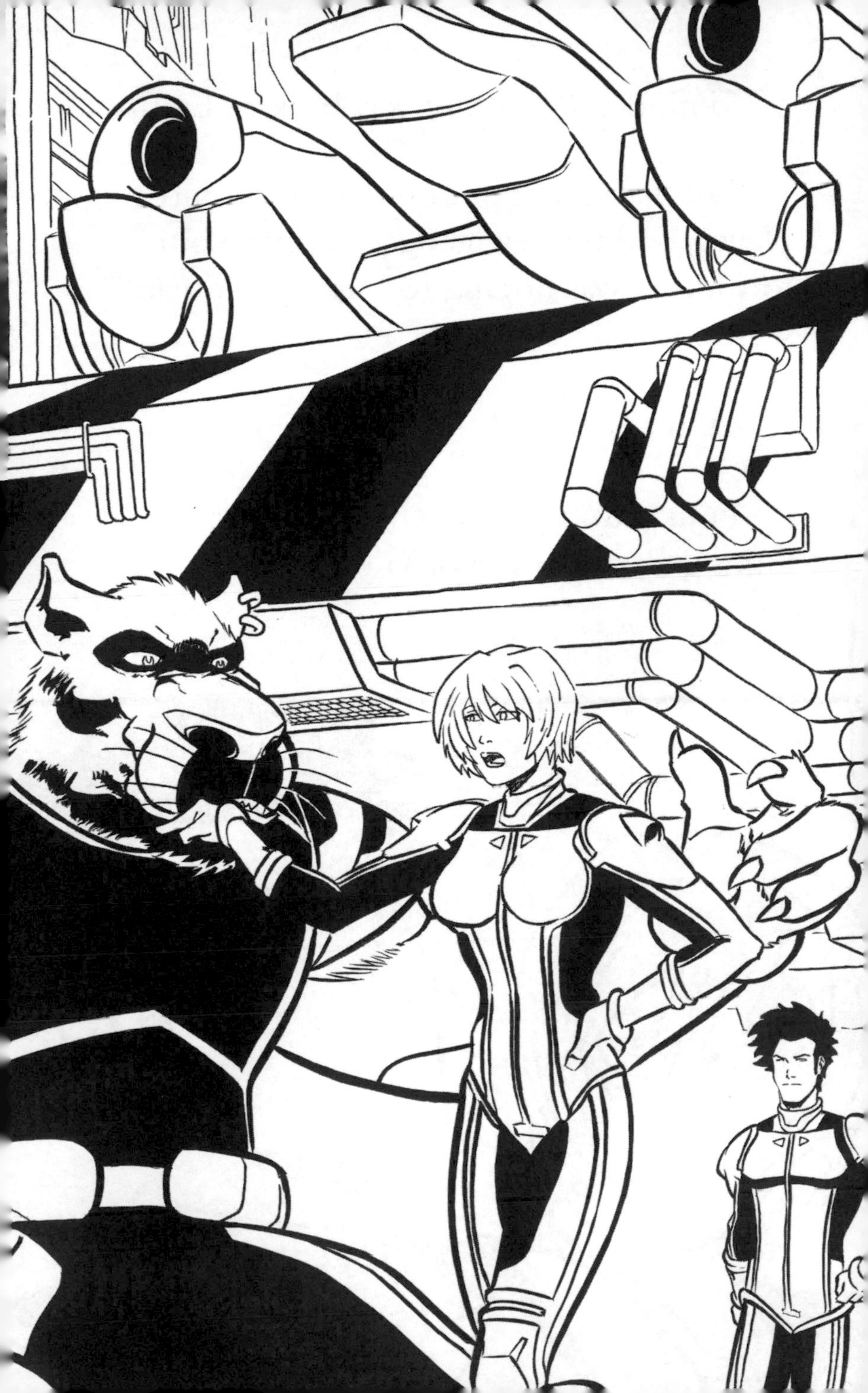

Finn moaned all the way back to Earth.

'All that time hunting around on those planets, and no new gadgets to make our fortunes! I was hoping to find the ultimate secret, Suma!'

'Actually, Finn, I think we did find it.'

Finn didn't know what Suma was talking about. But Misha did.